Happy Beachcombing!

What the Sea Left Behind

written and illustrated by

Mimi Gregoire Carpenter

mimi gregoire carpenter

10/6/2000

Down East Books
Camden, Maine 04843

Hi! Just call me Tessa. I live in the rugged state of Maine, along the Atlantic ocean. My mom and I are artists. We like to paint the things the sea leaves behind.

She and I go out and look for things when the weather is good and the sun is shining any time of the year. You might miss the things we look for, but ... if you look carefully, you will see.

M. Gregoire Carpenter '78

I like to take the ferry out to Islesboro. We collect the little pebbles that are rolled and tossed and polished by the tide in the horseshoe beach. They are round and smooth and shiny. Some days I collect just the black ones with stripes. On another day I might choose the yellow, or the green, or the white. There are so many . . .

... so many that sometimes, even though I'm tired, I just don't know how to stop. I play a game with myself. If I find a red pebble, I pretend that I have found a special jewel, a reward, and then I don't have to search anymore.

Near the smooth pebbles, there are old and rough pebbles and pieces of driftwood.

Mimi-Gregoire Carpenter '18

Mimi Gregoire Carpenter '79

I like to use my imagination and wonder about where things in the cove come from. A piece of metal could have come from a tugboat, an old car, or maybe just a pipe from someone's cottage.

Exploring the beach at Pemaquid is my favorite kind of adventure. Sometimes things seem scary. At first a piece of seaweed looks like a mask, spooky eyes looking through a rubbery face.

Mimi Gregoire Carpenter '80

My mommy read me the story THE BEAUTY AND THE BEAST. We talked about how the things in the sea are like the beast in the story. At first they seem ugly, but if you look closely and you are not afraid of them, they are really quite beautiful in a special way. Look at the rockweed, irish moss, the dulce, and the sea lettuce and the oarweed.

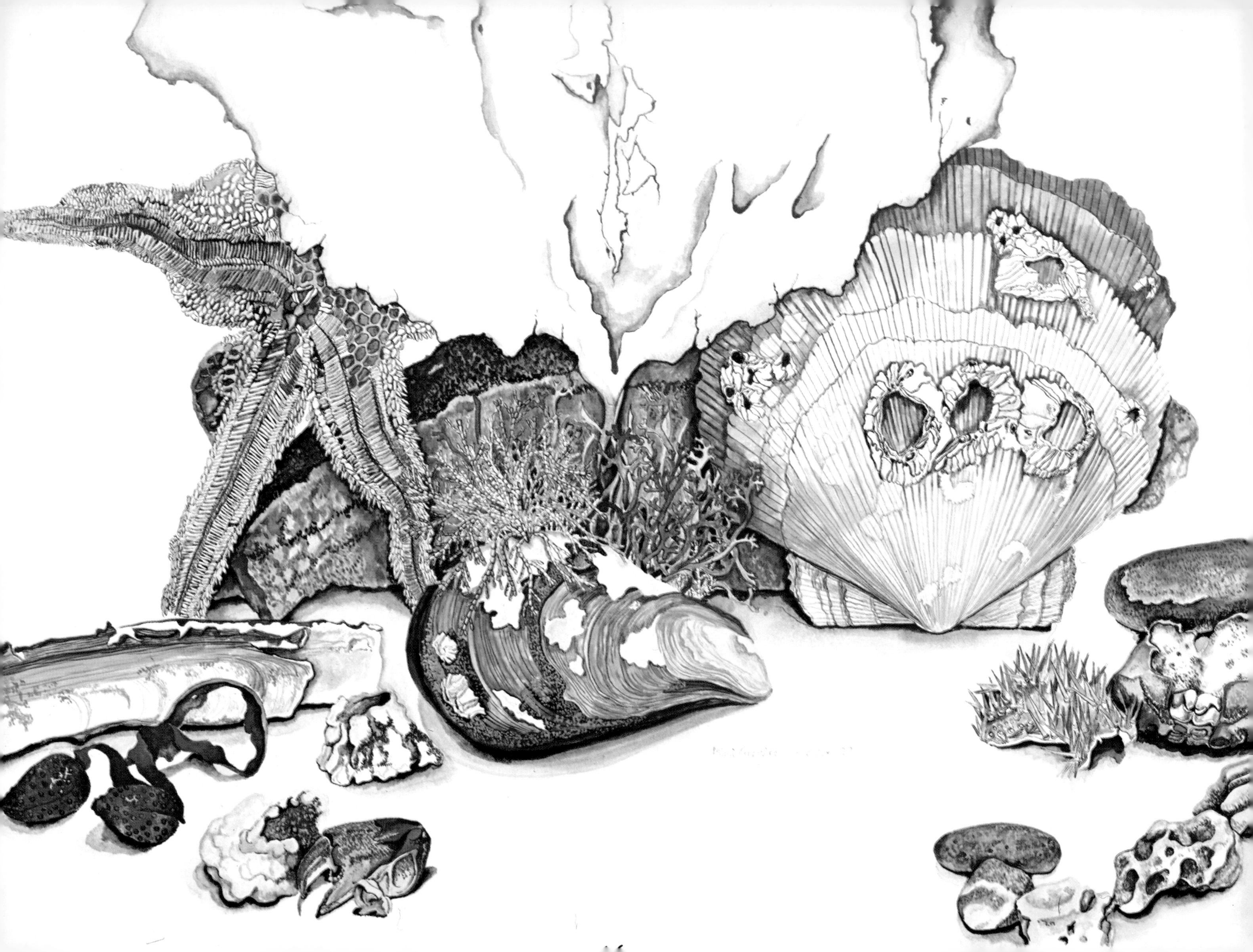

Look closely at a piece of seaweed, or a scallop shell covered with barnacles, or a dried up starfish. Maybe if you try looking at these things in a different way, the things you used to ignore or look away from will seem more special to you and what you used to think of as ugly will change.

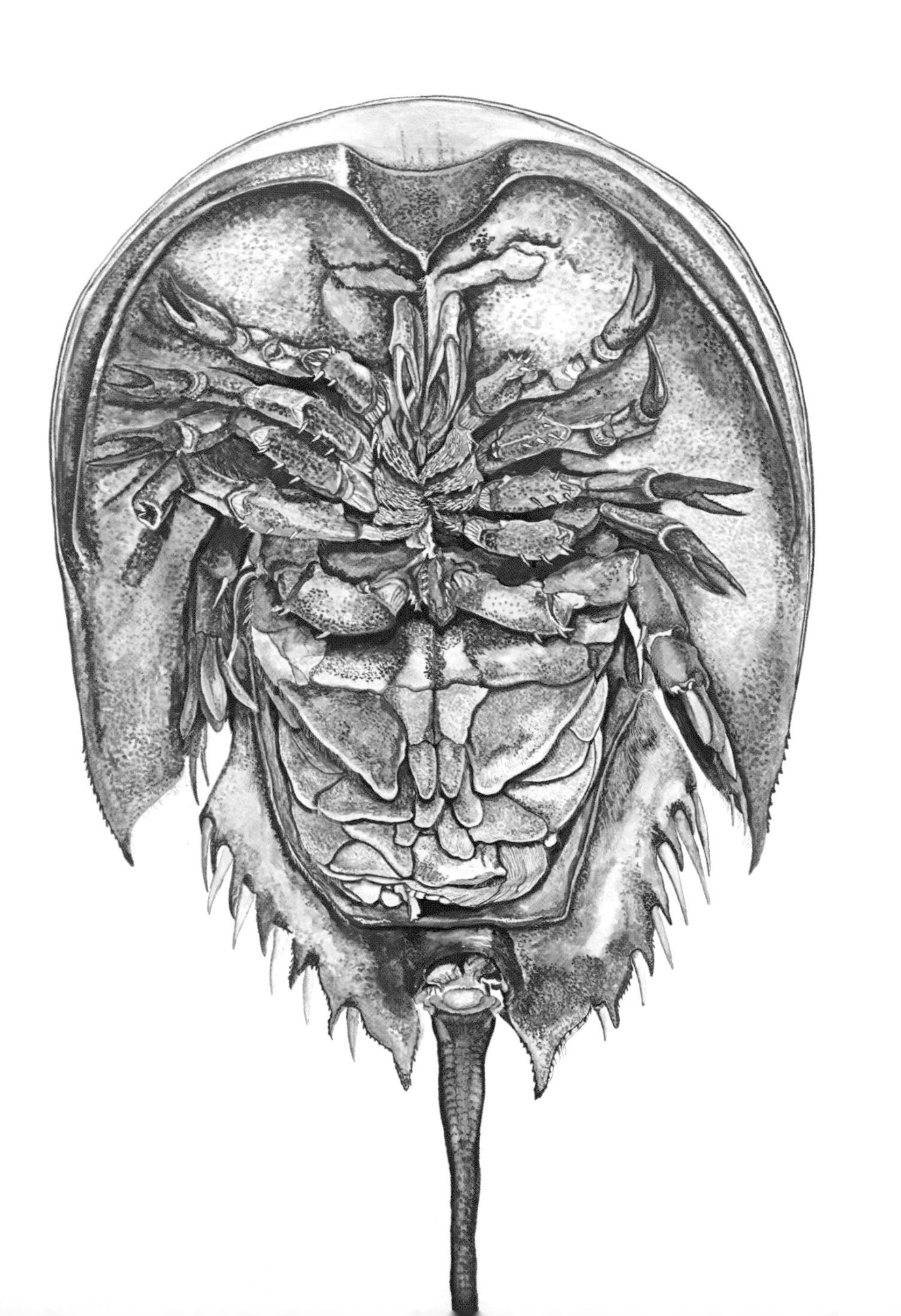

Along the marshes of the river in Damariscotta, there are papery thin horse-shoe crabs to pick up. I would never kick at one or toss it away. It washed up there especially for me and I can hang it on my wall.

I find razor clams, long and white, on the beach too. They look more like knives to me, but I can draw in the sand with them.

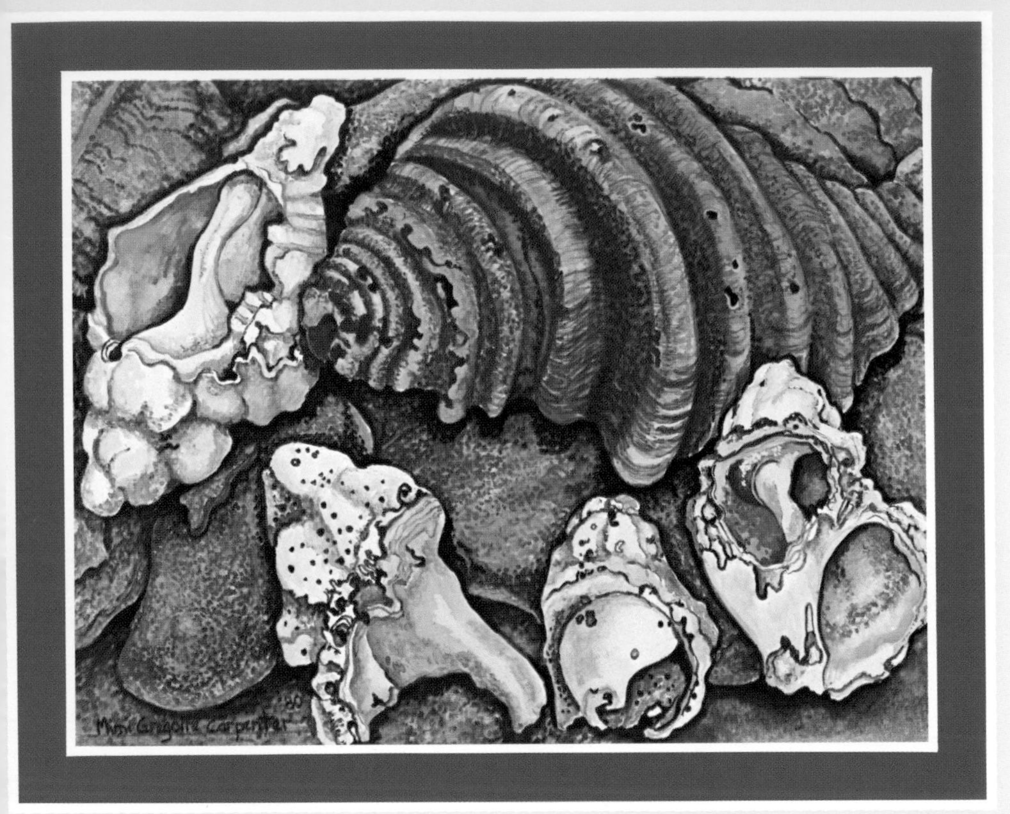

When I explore the rocks at Pemaquid Point, I'm certain not to save only the unbroken and shiny shells. I save them all. Each one is special . . . if you look carefully.

Watch the hungry seagulls find sea urchins. They pick them up and drop them on the rocks as they swoop by breaking the shells and eating the good food inside. When I walk along the rocks I find many broken urchins, with and without spines. The spines get worn off as they fall or by the wind and the water.

I look closely . . .

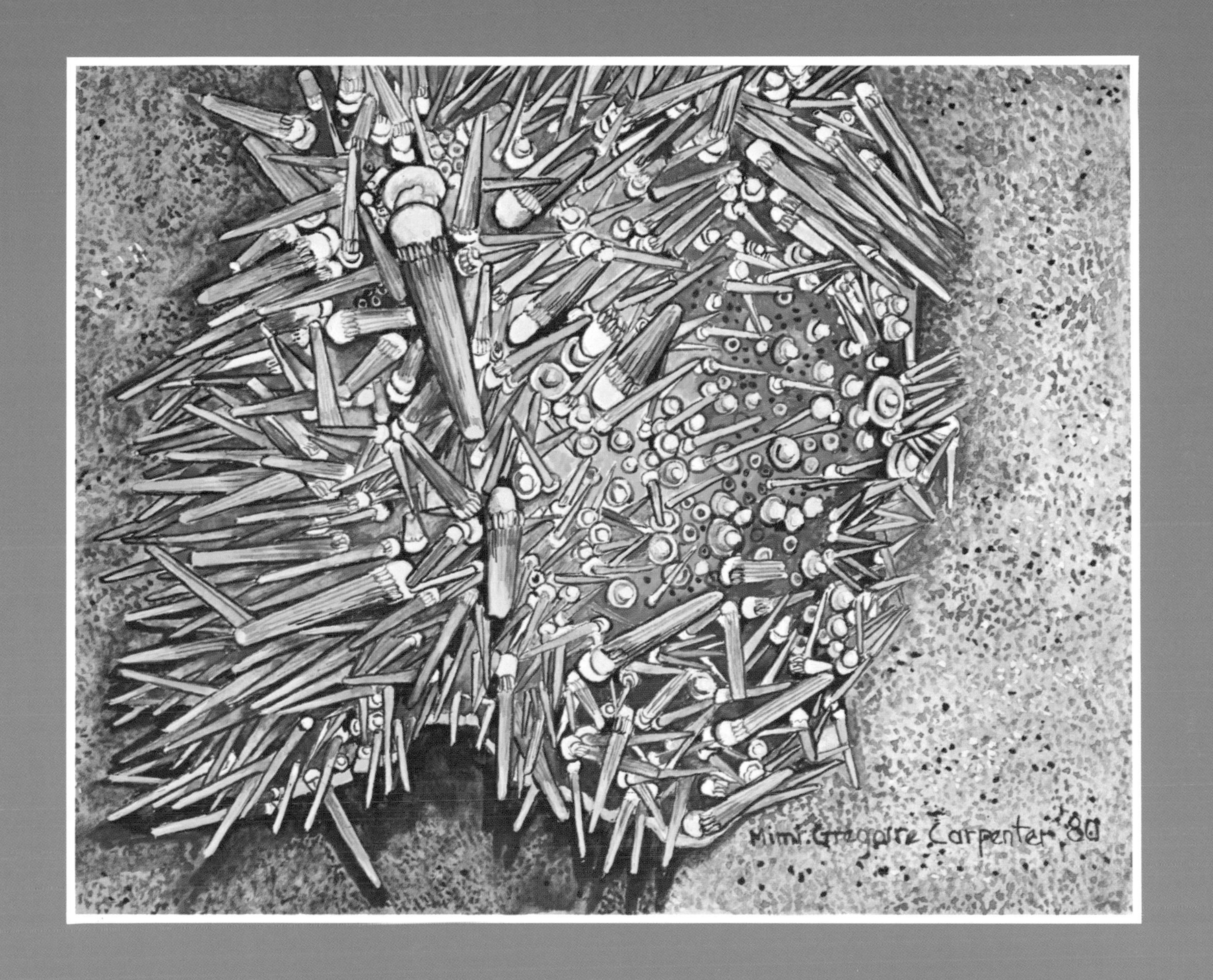

even more closely.

Seagulls eat the many little crabs that rush around in the tidal pools too. I find all kinds of claws and empty crab bodies, big and little. Some are purple, some are orange or green. Sometimes they are all in one piece and sometimes they are in many pieces.

I like to fill my cup with snails and periwinkles. Whenever I can't find anything else, I know that I can always find plenty of snails, gray or brown, white or yellow. There are curly whelks, striped snails and limpets. I have to be careful not to choose any live ones to put in my cup, just the outside skeletons.

There are other skeletons in the rocks. Purple and blue mussels covered with white or pink rock crust. Living things called branching corallina, hook themselves

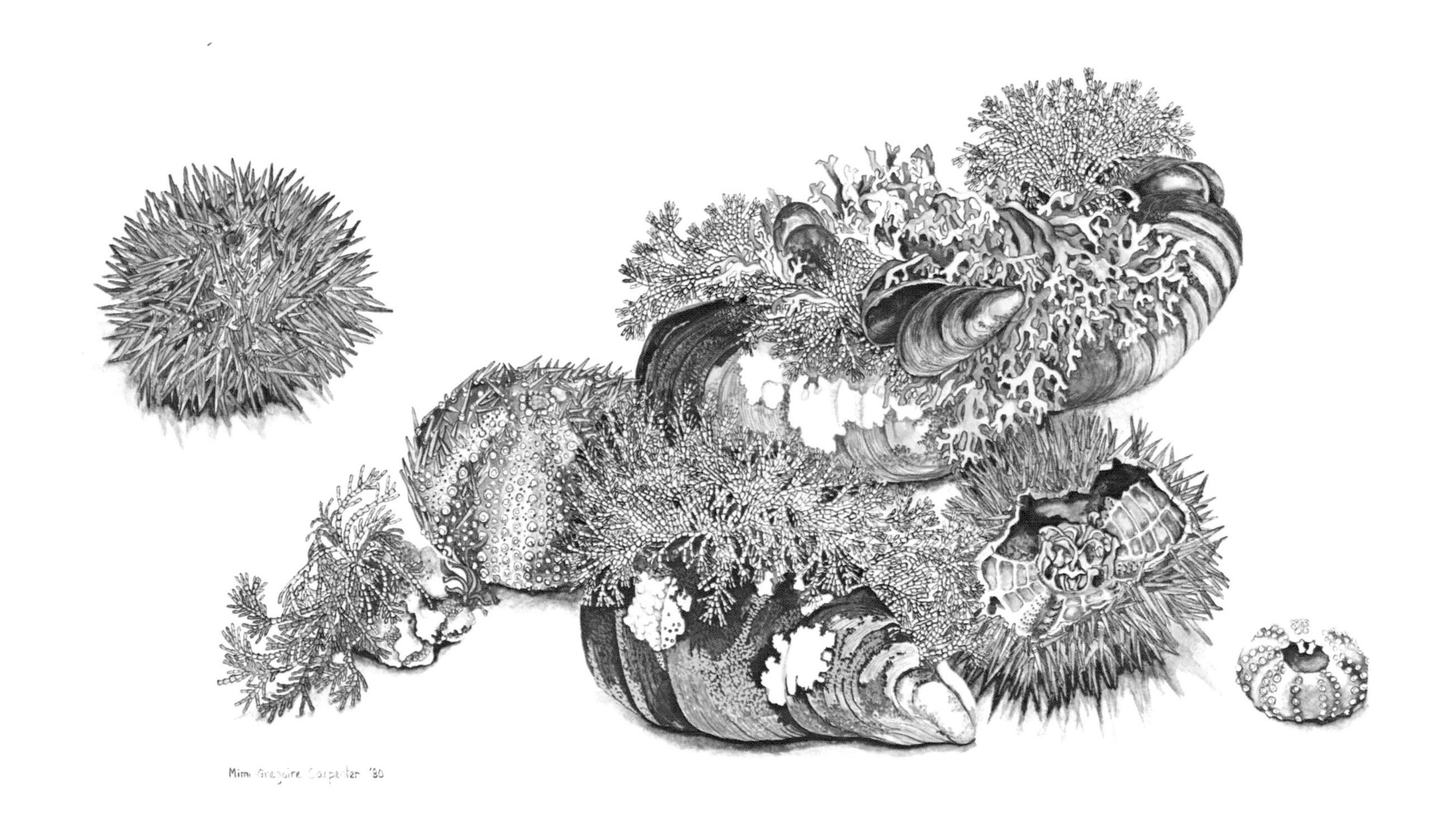

onto the mussels. The tiny pink branches grow, die, and are bleached by the salt in the ocean water. They break even when I pick them up carefully.

The oarweed holds on tightly when the waves try to pull them away from the mussel shells.

At the end of the day, after we have gathered all the things that the sea has left behind, we like to have a feast of lobster in New Harbor. But I'm most excited when I've finished eating because I will have more to add to my collection...

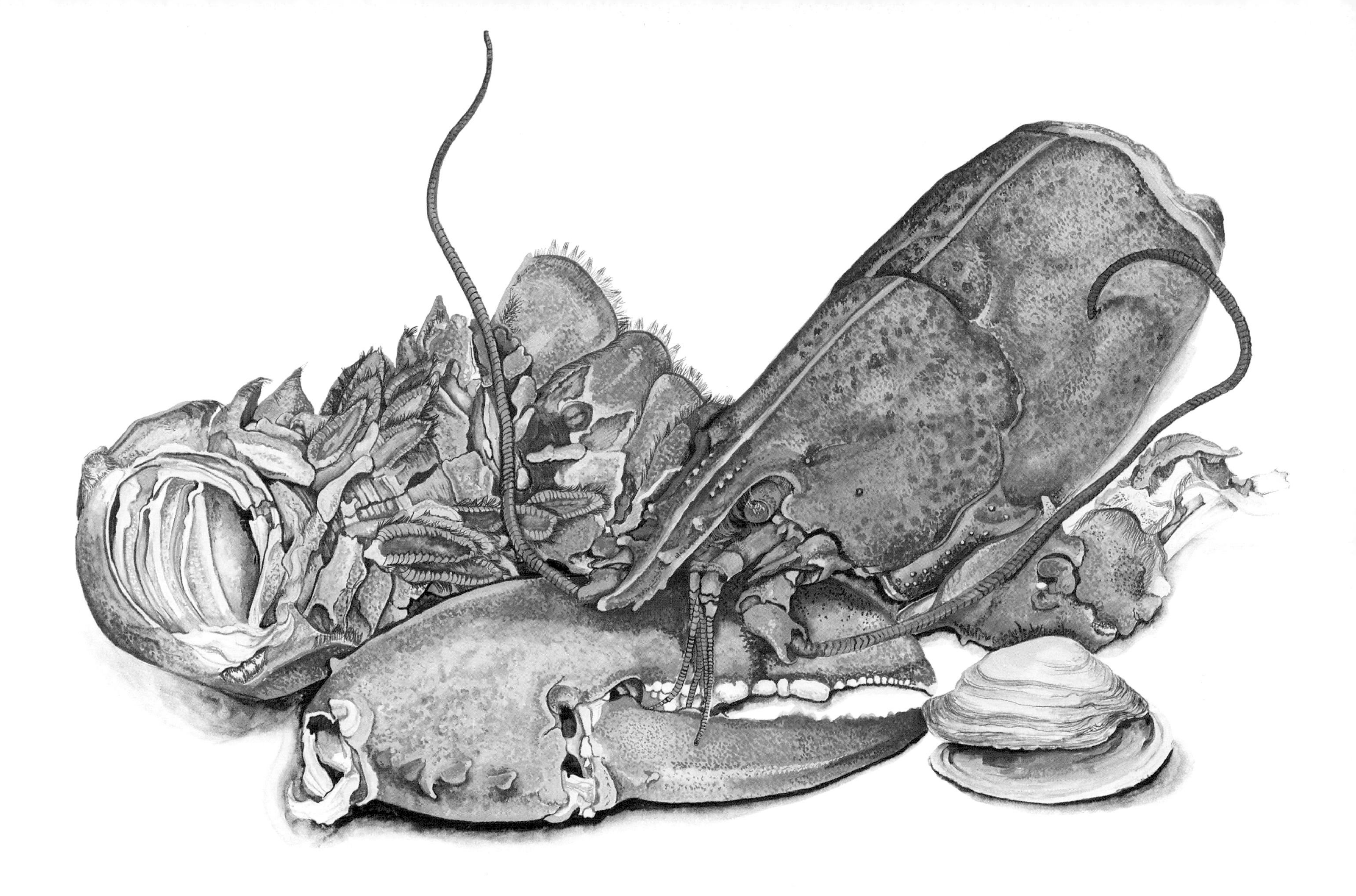

lobster shells.

Now I can get out all my art supplies. I can draw or paint, make collages or clay forms, even when the sun isn't shining and I can't be at the ocean anymore.

Your turn!

Now you can do some collecting. If you're not lucky enough to visit the ocean or live in Maine like me, there are many other things to collect - things that you might not have noticed before.

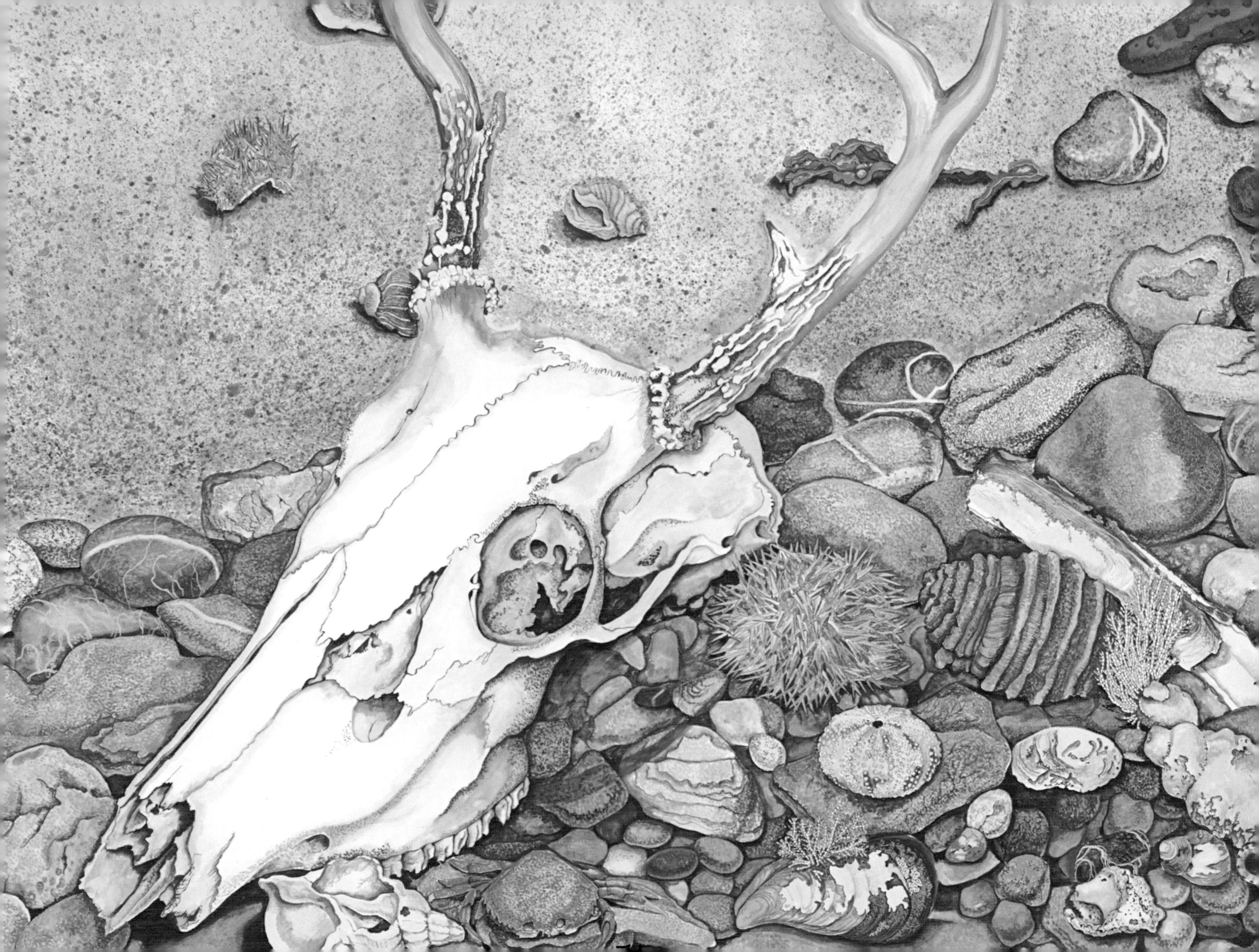